Humphrey's

Corner

*To Georgie, Ralph and Kim,
love Mummy x*

VIKING

Published by the Penguin Group
Penguin Books Ltd, 27 Wrights Lane, London W8 5TZ, England
Penguin Putnam Inc., 375 Hudson Street, New York, New York 10014, USA
Penguin Books Australia Ltd, Ringwood, Victoria, Australia
Penguin Books Canada Ltd, 10 Alcorn Avenue, Toronto, Ontario, Canada M4V 3B2
Penguin Books (NZ) Ltd, Private Bag 102902, NSMC, Auckland, New Zealand

On the World Wide Web at: www.penguin.com

Penguin Books Ltd, Registered Offices: Harmondsworth, Middlesex, England

First published 1999
5 7 9 10 8 6

Copyright © Sally Hunter, 1999

Printed at Oriental Press, Dubai, U. A. E.

British Library Cataloguing in Publication Data
A CIP catalogue record for this book is available from the British Library

This edition produced for The Book People Ltd, Hall Wood Avenue,
Haydock, St Helens WA 9UL

ISBN 0-670-88636-X

Humphrey's

Corner

Sally Hunter

TED SMART

Humphrey was looking for Mop.
He wanted to go and play
but he had to have Mop
otherwise it just wasn't right.

Humphrey found Mop
and his Mooey
squashed down the
side of the bed.

He thought the
stool might be
useful as well.

So Humphrey put
his Mooey
and the little stool
into a box
with Mop on top
(so he could see where he was going)…

Humphrey

and went to find somewhere interesting to play.

He found some pretty colours...

...sploshy sounds...

and a house for Mop.

Mop was poorly and needed his medicine...

but the floor was a bit hard
and there was sticky
stuff everywhere.

It wasn't quite right.

So Humphrey put
his Mooey,
the little stool
and the bottle with pretty colours
into the box
with Mop on top...

and walked away to look for somewhere cosy to play.

Humphrey peeped in.
It was all pink and sunny...

...and smelled just like Mummy...

... with lots of

very pretty things

to look at.

Mop was in a boat sailing
in a sparkly blue sea...

but it was a bit dark
and very quiet.

It wasn't quite right.

So Humphrey put
his Mooey,
the little stool,
the bottle with the pretty colours
and Mummy's sparkly necklace
into the box
with Mop on top...

and walked away to look for somewhere
different to play.

He found a very nice hidey hole.

Mop needed
his afternoon rest ...

but there were lots
of gurgly, clanky noises.

Mop said he was too hot.

It wasn't quite right.

So Humphrey put
his Mooey,
the little stool,
the bottle with the pretty colours,
Mummy's sparkly necklace
and his favourite towel with the ducks on
into the box
with Mop on top...

and walked away to look for somewhere else
to play.

Humphrey had a
bit of a problem
with the stairs...

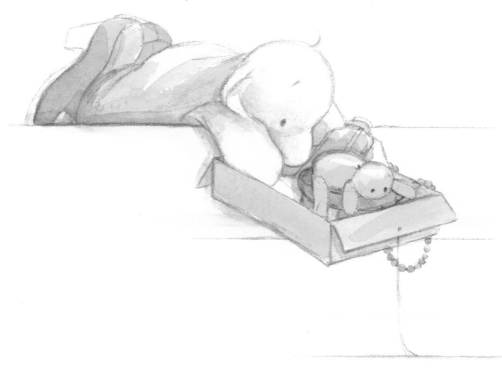

and his box...

... and because Mop was on the top he fell,

flop,

plop,

down the stairs.

Humphrey wanted to fetch
Mop, but he couldn't leave his
box in case that fell too.

He suddenly felt tired
and didn't want to play any more.

"Are you all right, little love?" asked Mummy.

Mummy picked up the box, gave Mop back
to Humphrey and helped them both downstairs.

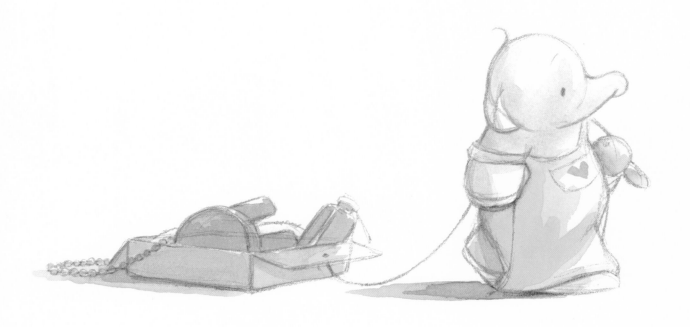

Humphrey followed Mummy into the kitchen.
It was lovely and warm...

... with nice things on the table ...

...and a very special place.

It was Humphrey's and Mop's
secret castle.
Mop was a king on his throne
with jewels and treasure.

It was very cosy...

...and near Mummy.

It was just right.